Leon Rosselson

Rosa's Singing Grandfather

Illustrated by Norman Young

PUFFIN BOOKS

For Yolanda, Ruth and Danielle
and in memory of Talya and of my father

PUFFIN BOOKS

Published by the Penguin Group
Penguin Books Ltd, 27 Wrights Lane, London W8 5TZ, England
Penguin Books USA Inc., 375 Hudson Street, New York, New York 10014, USA
Penguin Books Australia Ltd, Ringwood, Victoria, Australia
Penguin Books Canada Ltd, 10 Alcorn Avenue, Toronto, Ontario, Canada M4V 3B2
Penguin Books (NZ) Ltd, 182–190 Wairau Road, Auckland 10, New Zealand

Penguin Books Ltd, Registered Offices: Harmondsworth, Middlesex, England

First published by Viking 1991
Published in Puffin Books 1992
10 9 8 7 6 5 4 3 2 1

Printed in England by Clays Ltd, St Ives plc
Filmset in Linotron Times

Contents

Remembering Grandma   7

How Grandfather Found His
    Voice   33

How Grandfather Lost His
    Fear of the Dark   53

Something Important   74

Remembering Grandma

"Are you going to stay with Sam this afternoon?" said Rosa's mum.

Sam was Rosa's friend who lived in the next street.

"What are you going to do?" said Rosa.

"I'm going with Grandad to put flowers on Grandma's grave."

"Why?" said Rosa.

"Cos she was my mum. Your grandmother. I told you. It's four years since she died. We always put flowers on her grave."

"Does she know?" asked Rosa. "Can she smell them?"

"I don't know," said her mum. "Maybe. Maybe not. Anyway, it's just to show that we remember her and miss her."

"I remember her," said Rosa.

"Do you? You were very small. What do you remember?"

8

"She made me raisin cakes,"
said Rosa.

Her mother laughed. "Trust
you to remember that, Rosa."

"And she had a beard."

"She did not," said her
mother indignantly.

"She did, cos she used to kiss
me with it."

"Well," said her mum, "I don't remember her ever having a beard."

"And her kitchen was always warm and smelt nice and sweet," said Rosa.

"That's true," said her mum. "It did." And Rosa saw her wipe a tear away from her cheek.

"Can I come?"

"Oh, Rosa, you don't want to come. You'll be happier with Sam."

"I remember her as well," said Rosa. "So I should put flowers on her grave."

Her mother looked doubtful. Then she said, "All right. Why not? You're old enough, after all. Only you've got to promise to be good and not badger me with questions while we're there. I couldn't cope with it."

Rosa promised. And dressed in their best clothes, they went off in the car to collect Grandad.

It was a bright sunny Sunday
afternoon in July. The
cemetery where Rosa's
grandmother was buried was a
little way out of town. They
walked from the car-park into

what looked to Rosa like an enormous field where hundreds of stone slabs were growing. Rosa wanted to ask what they were for, but she didn't dare. She was carrying a little bunch of orange marigolds. Her mother held some lilies and Grandad six red roses.

Her mother and grandfather hesitated as they entered the cemetery and looked at each other.

"We always do this," said her mother. "Every time. It's awful."

"They all look the same," said Grandfather. "And there

are more of them."

"More graves," said her mother. "Come on, I think I remember."

Rosa followed them as they threaded their way through lines of gravestones. Some of the stones were old and some were shiny-new, and they all had writing on them. Rosa wondered why but didn't dare ask. She saw, too, that some of the graves were grass and some earth and some had jars or little pots of flowers on them.

"Here it is," said her mother.

They stopped in front of a

grassy grave. The writing on the stone was clear and Rosa could almost read it.

In loving memory, it said. Emma Shenstone, died aged 70. Much missed by her husband and family.

Rosa put her flowers on the grave like her mother and

grandfather. Then they stood for a moment in silence.

"Don't sing," muttered her mother. "Please don't sing."

But he did, of course. Rosa had never heard him sing this

song before and she wondered why her mother hadn't wanted him to sing it. He sang it sadly and quite quietly so as not to disturb the other people in the cemetery or under the earth, but loudly enough, Rosa thought, for her grandmother to hear. This is what he sang:

"The winter may pass and the
    spring fade away, the spring
    fade away,
The summer flowers may
    wither, the autumn leaves
    decay, the autumn leaves
    decay,
But though the time be weary,

I know thou wilt come, I
   know thou wilt come,
And faithful to my promise, I'll
   wait for thee at home,
I'll wait for thee at home . . ."

Afterwards, Rosa took
Grandfather back to her house

for tea. While her mum was in the kitchen, she tried to get Grandad to play cards with her, but he kept forgetting whose turn it was so she gave up.

"Sing that song, Grandad. The one you sang at Grandma's grave."

"Oh no, little one. I couldn't do that."

"Why not, Grandad?"

"It's a special song. I only ever sang it to your grandma. It was her favourite."

"Do you think she could hear you?" asked Rosa.

"Well," said her

grandfather, "what do you think?"

"Maybe," said Rosa. "Maybe not."

"That's about it," he said. "Anyway, when I sing it, I remember your grandma and all the good times we had together. That's why I sing it. To remind me."

"What do you remember?" asked Rosa.

"Raisin cakes," he said. "She used to make delicious raisin cakes."

"Trust you to remember that, Grandad," said Rosa.

"And," Grandad went on, as

if he hadn't heard Rosa, "I remember when we first met."

"When was that, Grandad?"

"When was what?" said Grandad.

"When you first met," said Rosa.

"Before you were thought of," he said. "Before even your mother was thought of. A long, long time ago before the war."

"What war?" asked Rosa.

"The war," said Grandad. "The second one. I don't remember much about the first one."

"What was it like in the war?" asked Rosa.

"Horrible," he said. "Things used to fall out of the sky."

"What sort of things?"

"Bombs and bits of metal and aeroplanes. Nasty things like that. Dangerous, it was."

There was a silence. Grandfather seemed to have quite forgotten where he was and what story he was telling.

"Grandad," said Rosa, "tell me about when you met Grandma."

"Oh yes," he said, "I'm glad you remembered. It was when I was working as a waiter in a big café. A singing waiter, of course. And an opera company

was coming to town, so I thought I'd go and see them on my night off. They were doing an opera called *The Marriage of Figaro*. Did I ever tell you about operas, Rosa?"

"Where everyone sings?"
she said.

"Where everyone sings all
the time," he said. "Yes."

"Just like you do, Grandad."

"Not quite as good as me,"
said Grandad, "but they do
their best. Well, in those days I
didn't understand much about

opera or any of those things, and I was high up in the gallery so I couldn't see or understand much about what was happening down on the stage. It was an opera called . . . now what was it called?"

"Something about figs," said Rosa.

"That's the one," said Grandfather. "*The Marriage of Figaro*. Everyone dressing up as everyone else. I couldn't make head or tail of it. Then right in the middle up came a tune that I knew. So, of course, I sang along just to help the poor old singer out: Now your

days of philandering are over,"
he sang. "Dum-di-dum,
dum-di-dum, dum-di-dum-dum.
The next thing I knew, what do
you think happened?"

"They asked you to join the
opera," said Rosa, "and
become a famous singer."

"No," said Grandad.

"Somebody hit me on top of the head with a programme. Whack! I turned round and saw the most beautiful woman I have ever seen. Lovely rosy cheeks and two little dimples."

"Like my mum," said Rosa.

"Just like your mum," he said. "The same big brown eyes. You've got them, too."

"Was that Grandma?" asked Rosa.

"That was Grandma," he replied. "You should have heard her tell me off. 'I haven't come here to hear you sing,' she said. 'If you want to sing,' she said, 'instead of listening, you go somewhere we can't hear you.' Was she cross!"

"My mum gets cross sometimes," said Rosa.

"That's the sort of cross she was," Grandad went on. "Anyway, everybody was shushing us, so I thought I'd better stop singing for the rest of the opera. But when it was over and everyone was clapping and shouting for more, I turned round and looked up into her beautiful brown eyes and said" – and here Grandfather stood up in his best Sunday suit and bowed to Rosa – "'I apologize for

disturbing you by singing
during the opera, but now it's
over, I hope you won't mind if
I sing a song just for you.' So I
did."

"Did you really, Grandad?"

"Certainly. Right there, standing up in the gallery, I sang the song you heard me sing at the cemetery."

"What did Grandma do?" asked Rosa, her eyes open wide.

"She went very red. And everybody was clapping and cheering and shouting for more. Only this time, they were clapping for me, not the singers down on the stage. Encore, encore, they shouted. And that's how I first met your grandma. We used to have a good laugh about it afterwards."

Just then Rosa's mother
came in with the tea things and
a plate of raisin cakes warm
from the oven. Rosa and
Grandfather had four each.

"They're just like
Grandma's," said Rosa.

"Delicious," said Grandad.
"I didn't know you

remembered how to make these."

"Lots of things you don't know," said Rosa's mum.

"One thing I do know," Grandad said to Rosa. "Your grandma's still around somewhere."

"Where?" asked Rosa.

"In your mum's raisin cakes," he said. "And in your big brown eyes." And he pinched Rosa's cheeks till they went quite red.

How Grandfather Found His Voice

On Tuesday afternoon,
Grandfather met Rosa from
school and took her home with
him for tea. He did this every
Tuesday and Thursday without
fail, because on those two days
Rosa's mother worked in a
hospital and wasn't home in
time to meet her. Rosa didn't
have a father. As far as she

could remember, she'd never
had a father.

"I've got something special
to show you today," said
Grandfather as they walked
hand in hand to his small,
ground-floor flat.

"What is it, Grandad? What
is it?"

"I'm not telling. But it's got four legs and whiskers."

"I know, I know," said Rosa, dancing with excitement. "It's kittens. Your Polly's had kittens. Polly's had kittens," she sang. "Polly's had kittens."

"Just one kitten," said Grandfather. "Well, just one kitten now, anyway. Poor little mite."

When they got to Grandfather's flat, Rosa rushed in shouting: "Where is it? Where is it? I want to see it."

"It's not an it," said Grandfather. "She's a she.

And she's in the broom cupboard."

And so she was, a tiny, furry, grey bundle in a shoe box, snuggling against her mother. She was so small and fast asleep that Rosa hardly dared breathe or move or make a sound.

"What are you going to call her, Grandad?" she whispered.

"Don't know," said Grandad. "What do you think she looks like?"

"Gravy," said Rosa. "Can we call her Gravy?"

Grandfather led Rosa into the kitchen. "Gravy, Gravy,

give me your answer, do," he sang. "Well, why not? We'll call her Gravy and see how she likes it. Come on, now. Boiled eggs for tea."

"I can boil eggs," said Rosa.

"You just lay the table," said Grandad. "I'm in charge here."

So Rosa put the plates and the teaspoons and the egg-cups on the table while Grandfather carefully pricked a hole at the end of each egg with a pin before he put them in boiling water. He sliced the brown bread and buttered it and cut up some tomato and cucumber,

and put the special cakes he'd
bought on his large old plate,
which was decorated with pink
roses. And all the while, he
was singing to himself, "Daisy,
Daisy, give me your answer,
do –"

"Why are you always
singing, Grandad?" asked
Rosa.

"Doesn't your mum sing?" asked Grandad.

"Sometimes," said Rosa. "When she's in a good mood. Not always."

"Well," said Grandfather as they sat down to have their tea, "do you know how many brothers and sisters I had?"

Rosa thought. "Five," she said at last.

"More," said Grandad.

"Fifteen," said Rosa.

"Four brothers and three sisters," said Grandad. "How many does that make?"

"Seven," said Rosa.

"Quite right. And with all

those children, do you think
anyone took any notice of a
little pipsqueak like me?"

"No," said Rosa.

"Not a blind bit of notice,"
Grandad went on. "Until –"

Then he stopped and stared at
Rosa as if he'd forgotten what
he was saying.

"Until what?" asked Rosa.

"You just eat your tea and
stop asking questions," said
Grandad. "Otherwise, all your
teeth might fall out. See
these," he said, opening his
mouth. "All mine.

Seventy-eight and all my own teeth. Well, nearly. That's because when I was your age, I never asked questions."

Rosa looked at him to see if he was joking. He had a toothy grin, so she laughed.

"Wouldn't have made any difference if I had asked questions," said Grandfather. "No one ever listened to me. Until one Friday, I was having my weekly bath in front of the fire in the kitchen. We didn't have a proper bath, of course, no taps with running hot and cold water and that sort of thing. And no one was taking any notice of me as usual. And the water was getting colder and colder. So I said, just to see what would happen, I said, as loud as I could, 'I can sing a song'."

"What did happen?" asked Rosa.

"Not much," said Grandfather. "All my brothers and sisters were fighting and playing and my mum was making supper and my dad poked his head over his paper and said, 'Did you hear what the little lad said?' He always called me the little lad because he couldn't remember my name. And my mum went on cooking and my brothers and sisters went on playing and fighting and my dad went on reading the paper.

"So I thought, I'll show them. And I opened my mouth and out came this voice I never knew I had. That did it. They were all amazed. They stopped what they were doing and gathered round the bath-tub and listened to me sing. Afterwards my dad asked for three cheers for the little lad."

Rosa clapped her hands excitedly. "What song did you sing?" she asked.

"It's funny you should ask
that," he said, "because I
remember it as if it was
yesterday. It was the one about
the kipper."

And he opened his arms and
mouth wide and sang:

"You should hold a kipper in
    one hand not two
And wave it while you're
    talking like the big shots do.
Never put your elbows on the
    table while you eat
But leave a little room for
    other folks to park their
    feet . . ."

Rosa joined in at the end
because she'd heard the song
hundreds of times before.
    "You'd better have the last
cake, Rosa," said Grandad.
    "Can I?" she said.
    "Since you've asked so
nicely," he said, "you might as

well." So she did.

"After that," Grandad said, "they took notice of me all right. They called me the little lad with the voice. And that's how I got where I am today," he said, laughing.

Later that evening, Rosa was in her own kitchen, watching her mother wash up the crockery left over from breakfast.

"Mum," said Rosa.

Rosa's mother didn't say anything, because she was thinking about what they were going to have for dinner the next day.

"Mum," said Rosa again.

"Isn't it time you went to bed?" said her mother as she dried her hands.

"Can I have a bath?" asked Rosa.

"What, now?" said her mother. "I must sew this button

on your dress and then there's
a programme I want to watch
on the telly. Anyway, it's too
late now and you had a bath
yesterday."

And she started to thread the
needle to sew the button on
Rosa's dress.

"Mum," said Rosa.

"Rosa," said her mum, "I thought I told you to get ready for bed."

"I can sing a song," said Rosa.

"I'm sure you can," said her mother absent-mindedly.

Rosa stood up and opened her arms and her mouth and began to sing:

"You should hold a kipper in
    one hand not two
And wave it while you're
    talking like the big shots
    do –"

Her mother looked at Rosa

as she sang, and when it came to the last line she joined in because she'd heard the song hundreds of times before.

"I haven't heard that in a long time," said Rosa's mother. Then suddenly she put down her sewing and picked up Rosa and kissed her.

"I do know you're here," she said to Rosa. "Even when I'm busy doing other things, I haven't forgotten you. How could I do that?" she said.

And she gave her a big hug.

How Grandfather Lost His Fear of the Dark

Rosa lived with her mother in a house that had been converted into two flats. They lived in the downstairs flat where Rosa had her own small bedroom, with her own little bed and her pictures and drawings on the walls and her blackboard and easel and toys and games and favourite teddy which she'd always had, ever since she could remember.

She went to sleep with a night-light on, which her mother switched off when Rosa was asleep. Rosa didn't like the darkness in her room. It made creaking sounds from the cupboards and the corners. Things that in the day were friendly and familiar, like the box for her toys, the giant panda on top of her cupboard, her dressing-gown on the back of the door, changed at night into strange, frightening shapes. They seemed to stare at her and whisper at her and

grow and swell into something
menacing that wanted to
swallow her up as she lay there
in bed, clutching her old teddy.
It was better with the
night-light on, but she still

liked her door to be open when she went to sleep, just in case.

"Grandad," said Rosa one rainy Sunday while they were waiting for Rosa's mum to make the dinner. They were sitting side by side on the settee.

"Yes, Rosa," sang Grandad.

"Are you frightened of the dark?"

"Well," he said, "it's funny you should ask that. Because when I was a nipper, I was terrified of the dark."

"Did you used to have a night-light when you went to bed?"

"Oh no," said Grandad, "never knew about such things. Anyway, there were five of us boys squeezed into that little room, three in my bed, two in the other, so I never had to feel frightened. But when I had to go out in the backyard at night, with the wind blowing and the bushes waving and the branches creaking and shadows lurking everywhere to leap out at me, that was different. That was frightening."

"Why did you have to go out in the backyard?" asked Rosa.

"Cos that's where our lavatory was," he said. "We didn't have one inside."

"Why, Grandad?"

"That's the way it was," he said, "for people like us. Of course, I used to pretend I wasn't frightened. Otherwise all my brothers and sisters would've laughed at me and pointed and called me cowardy-custard. But many's the time I nearly wet myself sooner than go out in the backyard when it was dark. That's how frightened I was."

Rosa giggled. She was glad that she, at least, had a lavatory right next to her bedroom.

"I'm a bit frightened of the dark," she said. "I used to be a lot frightened. Then my mum came in and gave me a hug and turned on the lights to show there was nothing to be frightened of. Now I'm only a bit frightened. But I do like the night-light on."

"Well, my little one," said Grandfather, "if you like, I'll tell you the secret of how I stopped being frightened of the dark. Because now I rather enjoy sitting in the dark. Sometimes I don't switch the lights on for hours in the evenings because I find it's so peaceful sitting in my rocking-chair, thinking and dreaming and letting the darkness grow over me."

Rosa shivered. "Aren't you frightened any more then?" she asked.

"Not since I discovered the secret," he said. "Do you want to know what it is?"

"Yes, please," said Rosa. "I won't tell anyone."

"Better not," said Grandad. "They wouldn't understand. Because there's a special song, you see."

"What is it, Grandad?"

"I made it up myself," he said importantly.

"What is it, Grandad?"

"It goes like this," he said. And he sang it to her quietly:

"Bingles and bangles and
   bongles and boo,
Jingles and jangles and
   tu-whit-tu-whoo,
Higgledy-piggledy fee fie and
   fang,
Flibberty-gibberty – BANG."

He sang the last word so loudly, Rosa was startled and nearly fell off the settee. She

looked at him and frowned.
"It's a funny song," she said.

"It is, yes," said her
grandfather. "That's not all of
it, of course. But that's the
most important bit."

"Does it work?" she asked.

"It worked for me," he said.

"Cos it's magic?"

"I think it could be. But you have to keep your eyes shut while you're singing it and only open them when you get to the BANG, which you must sing very loudly to ward off the evil spirits." And he shut his eyes and began to sing again:

"Bingles and bangles and bongles and boo –"

Rosa shut her eyes and tried to join in, but her voice trailed behind his and her tongue tripped up over the bangles and the jangles and the fee and fang. But when they got to the

BANG, she joined in with all
her voice and opened her eyes
and looked at her grandfather
and laughed. He grinned and
wagged his finger at her and
sang on:

"When you feel nothingness
   waiting to swallow you,

Prickles that tear at you,
    nettles that sting,
When you hear footsteps that
    follow you, follow you,
This is the song you must sing –"

And this time Rosa joined in
with nearly all the funny
chorus and sang the BANG
even more loudly and opened
her eyes and laughed again.
And still Grandad, wagging his
finger, sang:

"When you see monsters
    lurking in doorways,
When you see shadows
    crouching to spring,
When you hear noises that
    scuttle in corners,
This is the song you must sing –
    "Bingles and bangles and
bongles and boo," they both
sang with their eyes shut. And

now they were both stepping,
hand in hand in the middle of
the room, in time to the rhythm
of the song. "Flibberty-
gibberty – B A N G," they sang
and opened their eyes to see
Rosa's mother standing in the
doorway looking at them,
open-mouthed.

"What on earth do you think
you're doing?" she asked.

"Grandad's teaching me
something," said Rosa, going
very red.

"He ought to know better at
his age," said her mother.
"Lay the table, please, Rosa."

"At my age," said

Grandfather with dignity, "if I can't have a bit of fun with my own little granddaughter, I don't know what I'm here for."

That evening, Rosa was in such a hurry to go to bed, her mother thought she must be sickening for something.

"I feel quite sleepy," said Rosa, yawning. "It's been such a long day."

And when she was tucked up in bed and Mum had finished telling her a story, she said, "You can close the door when you go out."

"Are you sure?" said her
mother.

"Just a little bit open," said
Rosa.

Her mother switched the
night-light on, kissed Rosa and
went out, leaving the door
slightly ajar. "Sweet dreams,"
she called.

Rosa looked around the room at the box in the corner and the panda on top of the cupboard and her dressing-gown behind the door. She closed her eyes and sang to herself:

"Bingles and bangles and
    bongles and boo,
Jingles and jangles and
    tu-whit-tu-whoo,
Higgledy-piggledy fee fie and
    fang,
Flibberty-gibberty – BANG."

She sang BANG more loudly and opened her eyes.

The panda was still sitting on top of the cupboard, looking quite friendly. The box was still the box. The dressing-gown on the door still looked like her dressing-gown. She shut her eyes and sang to herself once more: "Bingles and bangles and bongles and boo –"

But before she could reach as far as the BANG, she was fast asleep.

Something Important

On Thursday, Rosa's mum met
Rosa from school.

"Where's Grandad?" asked
Rosa.

"I forgot to tell you," said
her mum. "Grandad had a
hospital appointment this
afternoon. They let me off
early so I could meet you
instead. Aren't you pleased to
see me?"

"I wanted to tell Grandad something important," said Rosa. "Why has he gone to hospital?"

"Something important," said Mum. "Now I wonder what that can be. Hurry up, Rosa.

I've parked the car where I shouldn't."

Rosa looked worried as she ran alongside her mother. "Why is Grandad in hospital?" she asked again. "Is he ill?"

"Just a bit of pain he's been having," said Mum. "So he's gone for an X-ray and a check-up. Just in case. Come on. In the car and I'll take you to see him now. Then you can tell him your something important."

They got in the car and Rosa's mum drove off just in time to escape a traffic warden who was walking towards them, looking very serious.

"Is he going to be in hospital a long time?" said Rosa.

"It depends," said her mum. "They'll have to see the X-ray. Maybe they'll let him come home straightaway. Then we can take him with us. Because he won't wait for the

ambulance and you know what the buses are like."

Rosa looked thoughtful. "Mum," she said.

"Yes, Rosa," said Mum.

"Is Grandad going to die?"

"Of course not," said her mum. "It's just a bit of pain. He'll live to be a hundred, don't you worry."

"When people die," said Rosa, "why do they go and live in a hole in the ground?"

"You do ask funny questions," said her mum.

The hospital was crowded and, for Rosa, a bit frightening. People sat in rows

in the waiting-room, reading
magazines and sometimes
sighing and looking at their
watches while porters and
nurses hurried in and out.

"Sit here," said Rosa's mum.

"I'll go and find out what's happened to Grandad. Have you got something to do?"

"I've got my crayons," said Rosa.

"Draw Grandad a picture then. And don't move from here. Do you hear me?"

"Don't worry," said a friendly nurse. "I'll keep an eye on her."

Rosa watched her mother hurry away. This hospital was the one where her mum worked as a medical secretary. So, Rosa thought to herself, she'd soon find out what had happened to Grandad.

Rosa took a box of crayons
and a sheet of drawing paper
from her school-bag. She put
the paper on a table, knelt on
the floor in front of the table
and began to draw. She drew a
big brown tree with red apples
and green leaves. Underneath
the tree she coloured it green

for the grass, and in the grass
she drew very carefully a mass
of flowers of all different
shapes and colours. She
worked so hard she quite
forgot where she was.

It took Rosa's mum a
quarter of an hour to find
Grandad. He was sitting in the
corner of a little cubicle,
wearing a dressing-gown and
looking very sorry for himself.

"How long have you been
here?" Rosa's mum asked him.

"Hours," he said. "They told
me to come in here and undress
for the X-ray."

"They must have forgotten

you," she said. "Typical. Why didn't you sing out or something? You're usually good at that."

"Didn't feel like it," he said.

"Well, feeling sorry for yourself won't do any good. Come on, let's go and find out why you haven't had the X-ray and when you can see the doctor."

It was more than an hour later when Rosa looked up from her drawing and saw her mum's black skirt and shiny black shoes in front of her. She hadn't been bored and had hardly noticed the time. She'd

coloured in the blue of the sky
and a red sun and some birds
flying. In the tree a squirrel
was sitting and on the grass a
cat and a dog were lying
peacefully. It was a beautiful
picture.

"What a lovely picture!"
said her mother.

"Where's Grandad?" asked Rosa.

"They're keeping him in for a few days. Nothing to worry about. It's just in case. Come on, put the crayons away. It's about time we went home, I think."

"Can't I give Grandad his picture?"

"Tomorrow," said her mother. "We'll come and see him tomorrow evening. You can give it to him then."

The next evening, Rosa's mum drove back to the hospital with Rosa. It was quieter than in the day and they found

Grandad in a small ward with
only one other person – an old
man with no hair, who was
propped up against the pillows
listening to the radio through a
pair of earphones. Grandfather
was reading a newspaper. He
looked up and smiled when
they came in. "I've been
waiting for you," he said.
"Thought you'd never come.
Sit yourselves down."

They gave him a kiss and sat
down, Rosa's mum on a chair
and Rosa on Grandad's bed.

"I brought you some
grapes," said Rosa's mum.

Rosa looked all around her.

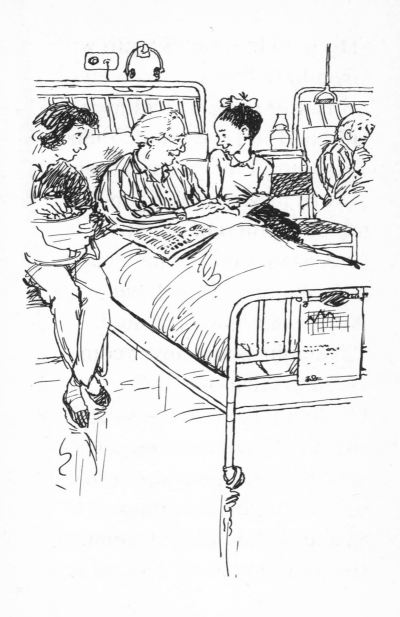

"Do you like it in hospital, Grandad?"

"Better than a holiday in the Hilton Hotel," he said. "The nurses are lovely. Only they're always fussing, taking my temperature and blood pressure every five minutes."

"You know they have to do that," said Rosa's mum. "They're taking care of you."

"Of course they are," said Grandad. "But it's not the same as being at home, is it?"

"I brought you a picture," said Rosa. "I did it myself." She gave Grandad the picture she'd drawn.

"That's beautiful," he said. "What a lovely peaceful spot. I like the cat and the dog. And the pretty flowers."

"You're there, too," said Rosa.

"I am? That's funny. There must be something the matter with my eyes, because I'm

blowed if I can see me. Where
am I?"

"There," said Rosa, pointing
at a patch of flowers and grass.
"Underneath the earth."

Grandfather blinked.
"Well," he said, "there's a
thing. Who would have
thought it? You've put me in a

peaceful place, all right, and if I end up there I should be happy enough. But maybe not for a little while yet, eh, Rosa?" And he pinched her cheek and grinned, showing all his teeth.

"Kiss your grandad goodbye," said Mum. "And then wait for me outside in the corridor. I just want a quick word."

Rosa did as she was told. She was jumping in and out of imaginary squares when her mother came out and took her hand.

"Time to go home," she

said. "You'll be late for bed."

As they were walking along the corridor to the exit, Rosa's mother said: "What about the something important you were going to tell Grandad yesterday?"

Rosa stopped suddenly. Her face went red. Then she turned and ran back down the corridor and into the ward and up to Grandad, lying in bed reading his paper. She stood on tiptoe and took a deep breath. Then she whispered in his ear. "I love you, Grandad," she whispered.

"Eh, what?" Grandad said.

"I love you, Grandad," she said more loudly. Then before he could recover from his surprise, she turned and ran back to her mother in the corridor.

They'd almost reached the
exit door when a familiar
voice, a strong voice, a singing
voice soared out of the ward
they'd just left and along the
corridor and, Rosa thought,

out through the door and into
the street and up into the sky
and everywhere.

"My love is a flower, all
    fragrant before me,
To soothe and restore me with
    wonderful art," sang the
    voice.

Two nurses walking along
towards them looked startled
and stopped to listen. "Loud
enough to wake the dead,"
said one.

"Yes," said the other, "but
what'll it do for the living?"

"Its charm and its power
So sweet and alluring

And always enduring
Will grow in my heart," sang
the voice.

"That's Grandad," said
Rosa happily.

"It certainly is," said her
mother.

"He's better, isn't he?" said
Rosa.

"He certainly is," said her
mother. And couldn't help
herself sweeping Rosa up and
giving her a big hug.

PUFFIN BOOKS

ROSA'S SINGING GRANDFATHER

Rosa's grandfather loves to sing! He has a special song for every time, place and problem to sing to Rosa. There is one for sorrow, one for joy, one for getting noticed, and even a secret one to stop Rosa from being scared of the dark.

These beautiful, gentle stories tell of the special friendship between Rosa and her singing grandfather.

Leon Rosselson is an established songwriter and performer whose songs have been widely recorded and popularized. He has two daughters and a granddaughter, and lives in London.